Disney's

DoUG™

Created by
Jim Jinkins

CHRONICLES

Doug Cheats

by Linda K. Garvey, Danny Campbell, and Kimberly Campbell

Illustrated by
William Presing and
Tony Curanaj

Doug Cheats is hand-illustrated by the same
Grade A Quality Jumbo artists who bring you
Disney's Doug, the television series.

JUMBO
PICTURES

GRADE A QUAL

D1468631

Disney
PRE

New York

Doug Cheats

CHAPTER ONE

"... so in 1218, Genghis Khan conquered Persia, becoming the most powerful ruler of eastern Asia," Chad Mayonnaise explained to his seventh grade history class at Beebe Bluff Middle School. Looking at the Khan's picture in his book, Doug Funnie drifted off, daydreaming.

Surveying his mighty empire,

Genghis Doug stood, arms folded across his chest. "Come, my dear," he spoke persuasively. "What good are riches and power if I cannot shower them on the one I love?"

Princess Patti's golden tresses glistened in the Asian sun. She looked amazed. "Me? You chose me? Oh, Genghis Doug, you're so . . . ruler-y!" she told him, awestruck.

Suddenly, Mr. Mayonnaise's voice broke into Doug's fantasy and he was back in history class. "And if you haven't started studying for this midterm exam by now, you will be in a lot of

trouble on Friday." Aw, man! Doug
thought, I'm doomed!

The bell rang. He picked up his
books and headed for his locker

with Skeeter. "Hey, man, have you started studying?" he asked his best human friend. "This test is gonna be hard!"

"No," honked Skeeter. "Nobody ever *really* starts studying that far ahead, but I'll start today when I get home. It's the kind of test you can't pass from just one night of cramming."

Doug traded his history book for *Living, Breathing Literature* and headed for Ms. Kristal's classroom. "Yeah, I know," he agreed. "That's what worries me. We've only got four days left."

"Yeah, and tonight's our Bluffscout awards ceremony. We

can't miss that. Then Thursday, we have that algebra test!"

Doug stopped right in Ms. Kristal's doorway. "Oh, no!" he cried. "I forgot about that!"

Skeeter pulled him to his desk. "Oh, I wouldn't worry about algebra, Doug. You've been doing your homework, right?" Doug nodded, and Skeeter continued, "Then you'll be okay. Those math rules—you either know 'em or you don't, honk, honk."

Class began and Ms. Kristal, dressed as a medieval English page, leaped onto her desk to grasp the sword planted there. Doug sank down in his seat.

Somehow, what Skeeter said
didn't make him feel better.

Doug left school that afternoon,
still worrying. He opened his
front door. His mother stood just
inside, holding her purse,

Dirtbike, and a wooden board.

"Oh, thank goodness, Douglas, you're here! How was your day, dear? I'm sorry to rush you, but I'm late for my Deja Vu board meeting." As she spoke, Theda Funnie kissed him on the cheek, handed him the baby, and headed out the door. "There's milk and cookies in the kitchen. I'll be back by six o'clock." And with that, she was gone.

CHAPTER TWO

Doug stood holding Dirtbike, who happily patted his cheek. He had forgotten all about promising to baby-sit. "Well," he said, "let's see what kind of cookies we have, Dirtbike. Then you can play with your toys while I study."

After Doug and Dirtbike polished off the cookies and milk, it was time to study. Doug got out

Dirtbike's favorite toys, but she wasn't interested. She immed- iately crawled to the garbage can and knocked it over. Doug caught her just before she bit Dad's old newspaper. Then, she pulled all the books off the shelf. As Doug put the books back in place, she reached the coffee table and began tugging on a vase of flowers. He

dove across the room to make a last-minute save. Dirtbike giggled and patted his face again. "This isn't working," he sighed.

He decided to hold Dirtbike to keep her out of trouble. She loved sitting on her big brother's lap. She also loved the big history book he wanted to read. She tried to eat the pages! Then, before he could read to the end of a sentence, she kicked the book off his lap and he had to start all over again.

But when she tried to tear the pages out, Doug finally gave up. "Dirtbike, what am I going to do with you?" he asked. "Wait a minute! Where's that video you like so much?" He looked around. "Here—*The Buckteeth Boys Creepy Crawlers*." He started the tape and put Dirtbike down. She clapped her hands and laughed when she saw her favorite show. And she stayed! Relieved, Doug opened his book.

One minute later, Doug was tapping his pencil to the music. He knew this tape almost as well as she did. Soon, he began to hum along. Before he realized it, Doug was singing the Buckteeth Boys theme.

The video was nearly over when Doug heard his mother's voice,

"I'm home!" He looked at his
watch and gasped, "It's ten to six!
That only leaves thirty minutes
to study!"

Doug rushed upstairs and
began to cram. Who was
Alexander the Great? When and
what did he rule? Who conquered
Greece—the Romans or the

Persians? Where is Persia, any-way?!

"Douglas," Theda Funnie called out. "Skeeter's here!"

"Oh, man!" Doug moaned, closing his history book and heading out the door.

CHAPTER THREE

Skeeter talked all the way next door to the Bluffscout meeting. "I can't wait, Doug! Mr. Dink's going to give both of us the Bluffscout Badge of Honor for Advanced Bird Stalking and Chipmunk Hostelry! Did you practice the secret Bluffscout salute for the awards ceremony?"

"No, I was kinda busy this afternoon," Doug answered.

"No sweat, man. It goes like this," Skeeter said, demonstrating the salute. Seconds later, his arms were hopelessly entangled. "I guess I shouldn't try to salute and walk at the same time, honk, honk."

Doug decided not to stay after the ceremony . . . just long enough for a bowl of Mr. Dink's chili fiesta olé. And, of course, one of Mayor Tippy's famous hot beety-banana fudge-nutty sundaes for dessert. He couldn't miss that!

At the party, everyone was

talking about the big test.
Everybody was nervous about it,
except Roger.

"I've got better things to do
than waste my time on some

lame-o test! What a bunch of losers!" cackled Roger.

"Well, there's a lot to remember!" Doug said defensively.

But he decided not to worry about it right now and have a hot beety-banana fudge-nutty sundae. Before he realized it, it was 9:30. He rushed home and studied for thirty minutes. Then he fell fast asleep.

CHAPTER FOUR

At school Tuesday, Doug spent
every minute studying history. He
hid his study pages in his note-
book and studied through all of
his other classes—except P.E. and
algebra, of course. Algebra was
the only class he was worse in
than history. But at least there
wasn't as much to memorize. And
Mr. Fort wasn't Patti's father.

In history class, Mr. Mayonnaise drilled everyone on exam questions. Doug wrote them all down. Alexander built the first library in Alexandria. The Phoenicians created the first alphabet. Facts piled up endlessly, and it all sounded vaguely familiar. It was all one big, confused jumble in his brain.

Roger leaned back in his seat, barely paying attention. "Roger," Mr. Mayonnaise warned, "this test is worth half your grade. I think you'd better take notes."

"Don't worry, Mr. Mayonnaise," Roger responded casually. "I'm ready for it!" Then he looked at Doug and said under his breath,

"You can be, too, Funnie. Five measly dollars will purchase this nifty little 'study guide.' My staff here," Roger indicated Willy and Boomer, "hacked into the school's computer and got the answer sheet. What do you say, Funnie?"

"No, Roger," Doug murmured. "I won't cheat."

"Suit yourself, loser!" Roger cackled.

Doug thought about Roger's offer. This test was going to be superhard. And he wanted to do well, especially in history. After all, Patti's dad was the teacher! He'd hate to look like a lamebrain.

In a flash, Doug saw himself riding at the helm of the *Santa Maria*, Princess Patti de May o' Naise poised elegantly beside him. "So you see, ma pretty Princess, soon we will reach India and bring back incredible riches!"

Suddenly, from the crow's nest, the lookout began to scream, "No, no! Captain Columbus! Ze world— she IS flat! We have come to ze edge! Turn back! Turn back!"

Princess Patti turned to the captain and said scornfully, "My daddy was right about you! The world is round, my foot! Well, genius, what do we do now?"

"Put her in reverse?"

Roars of laughter brought Doug back to history class in a hurry.

"What was that, Doug?" Mr. Mayonnaise smiled helpfully. "How did the Romans respond to Julius Caesar's love for Cleopatra?"

Horrified, Doug realized how he had answered the question: "Put her in reverse!"

He tried again. "Uh, sorry, sir. They, um, didn't like her much."

Aw, man! Doug thought, sliding down in his seat. Now I *really* need a good grade, just so Patti's dad won't think I'm not smart enough for his perfect daughter!

CHAPTER FIVE

As soon as Doug got home that afternoon, he opened his algebra book. Skeeter was right about one thing. You had to keep up to understand math. Doug flipped through several pages. "Oh, man!" he groaned out loud. "Skeet sure was wrong about this part. There are *lots* of formulas! I'll be memorizing these for hours," he whined as Porkchop came into his room.

Porkchop made a sympathetic "aw, man" noise and offered him a plate of sugar-fried beet-skins. A card was on top. Doug picked it up. "Oh, yeah, you mentioned this last week." He read aloud: "'The first graduating class of Puppy Palace's School of Canine Cuisine requests your presence at commencement. Top dog address: Porkchop Funnie.' Wow, Porkchop, you must be really good! When is this?"

Porkchop pointed to the card

in Doug's hand. "Thursday
evening . . ." Doug's face fell.
"Oh, no, Porkchop! Not *this*
Thursday. That's a terrible time!
I . . ."

As Doug spoke, Porkchop

gasped and his whole body sagged. Doug knew that he could not, for any reason, let his best nonhuman friend down. He picked up the sentence where he had left off. ". . . will just have to study some other time. I couldn't miss your speech." He smiled weakly. Porkchop gave him a big hug and offered him another beet-skin. Doug sighed, took the treat, and looked back at his algebra book.

It was late when he finished studying formulas. His head reeled with numbers, but he had to spend some time on history before bed. He barely got

past the first page when he
fell asleep right on top of the
covers.

CHAPTER SIX

Wednesday, Doug finished the
math exam before the bell rang.
Roger joined him in the hallway.
"So, Funnie, how'd you do? Didja
break any Class Doof records?"
Doug answered coolly, "Actually,
Roger, I think I did pretty good. I
studied a lot last night."

"Yeah, I bet," Roger replied.
"Right after you finished studying

for the history exam so you can impress Ms. Mayonnaise's dad!"

Instantly, Doug's confidence left. "Um, yeah, r-r-right after," he stammered.

Roger knew he'd hit a nerve. "What's the matter, Funnie? Still nervous about that test? I've got the answers you need, right here. I'll even give you a discount since we're so close to D day."

Doug thought for a minute. He knew it was wrong, but this time he really was in a jam. Besides, other people did it all the time. Like Roger!

But what if he got caught? That would be too humiliating! Patti

would probably hate him forever! And besides, cheating was wrong. He knew that.

"Come on, Funnie. I can't wait all day! Do you want it or not?" Roger asked impatiently.

"N-no, Roger, I'm not going to do it!"

"Okay, Funnie. It's *your* love life!"

Discouraged, Doug watched him go to his locker. I may not ace this test, he thought, but maybe I won't flunk. This afternoon and tonight, I'm gonna really knuckle down and study! I'll show him. I'll show everybody! I am NOT a doof!

CHAPTER SEVEN

"Douglas!" Mom called. "Time for dinner!"

Proud of himself, Doug went downstairs. He had come straight home and studied hard for two whole hours. Good thing, too, since tomorrow was Porkchop's graduation and the test was the next day. There was no time to waste.

After dinner, Doug heard Porkchop in the den, watching *Dr. Cop*. Aw, man! He had forgotten about the *Dr. Cop* marathon. "Four hours of fun-filled special effects!" the ads had promised. Doug had been waiting for this night for three weeks. Now he couldn't even watch it.

I'll just watch a few minutes, he thought, and then go study.

Two hours later, as the closing music played, Doug looked at his watch. Nine o'clock! He had stayed a lot longer than a couple of minutes. He raced upstairs to squeeze in an hour before bed-time.

But Doug's head was swimming with dates and names. "I just can't memorize all this stuff!" he complained to Porkchop, who had come in with a flaming plate and a fork. Porkchop doused the flame with a fire extinguisher and handed the plate to Doug.

"What's this?" Doug asked. Porkchop pointed to a recipe card that read Custard's Last Flan.

The two pals polished off the delicacy while Doug continued to grumble, until Mom knocked on his door. "Douglas? Lights out, dear."

Depressed, Doug turned out the lights. He had squandered another day.

CHAPTER EIGHT

"I haven't studied nearly enough," Doug told Skeeter on Thursday. "And there's only one more day!"

"Gee, man," Skeeter suggested, "just tell Porkchop you can't go."

"I guess I'll have to," Doug agreed.

After school, Porkchop met him at the front door with a home-made card. "Doug—Dog's Best

Friend," it read. Inside, it said,
"With me, you're always barking
up the right tree!" Porkchop
hugged Doug, whimpered a little,
and gave him a carnation for his
lapel. Then he led Doug upstairs
where he'd laid out his suit and
the tie with the bone theme.

How could Doug let him down
after all that? Doug decided to go
to graduation. When he got back,
he'd still have a couple of good
studying hours.

Graduation was incredible!
They feasted from the moment
they walked in. By the time they
went home, they were stuffed
with delicious gourmet food.

But Doug was determined to study. He drank some seltzer and went upstairs. An hour later, Mom knocked on his door. He begged to study a little longer, and she finally agreed. But he couldn't keep his eyes open. He conked out over his desk in thirty minutes, and he didn't even wake up when his dad put him to bed.

CHAPTER NINE

At 6:30 Friday morning, Doug's
eyes popped open. "Oh, no!" he
cried, immediately thinking about
the exam. "I've got to study!"
Panicked, he jumped out of bed
and dressed in record time,
nearly an hour before leaving for
school.

Between classes, Roger kept

after him about the test. Doug thought hard, but he could hear his father's voice in his head, saying, "You know, Mister, cheating is wrong. You only end up cheating yourself. Don't disappoint me like that, Doug."

But what about the test? He wasn't ready for it, and it was going to be hard! Patti's father would really be impressed if he made a good grade, and he'd probably say some nice things to her about how smart he was, *if* he aced it. And this answer sheet would help him.

Doug decided to do it! He was

sure he could get away with it.
After all, Roger did it all the time.
Just this once, he was going to
cheat.

CHAPTER TEN

Doug walked into history class exhilarated and determined. He looked at the paper he'd bought from Roger. "Midterm Exam Key: Seventh Grade History Class." There were 150 answers marked with A, B, C, or D for the first half. Short answers were listed for the rest. This was it, all right!

Doug placed the sheet in his chair and sat on it as Mr. Mayonnaise came in. "Good afternoon, class," he said, handing out the tests. "I hope you're prepared. These are the most challenging questions I could think of, but you are such good students, I know you'll do well. All I expect is your best."

Doug's stomach tightened. Mr. Mayonnaise turned around, and Doug quickly jerked

the key out and placed it under
his test.

Mr. Mayonnaise said, "You may
begin."

Doug sweated bullets as Patti's
father looked over his class. Mr.
Mayonnaise asked, "Doug, are you
all right?"

"Who, me?" Doug jumped. "Uh,
sure, sir. "I'm just . . . thinking."

Mr. Mayonnaise smiled. "I'm sure you'll do well, Doug. We went over this in class."

Maybe this isn't such a good idea, Doug thought. Maybe I should take my chances on what I already know.

He looked at the first question. "What did Julius Caesar mean when he said, 'Veni, vidi, vici'?

> (A) I name this salad 'Caesar!'
> (B) See ya later, alligator!
> (C) I came, I saw, I conquered.
> (D) Friends, Romans, country men, lend me your ears."

Oh, man, Doug thought, I need this key bad!

He slipped it out and looked at the first answer. "B." Hey, wait a minute! he thought. He wasn't sure what the right answer was, but he was certain that *Veni, vidi, vici* did *not* mean "See ya later, alligator!"

After looking at the second multiple-choice answer, Doug knew something was wrong. Canton, Ohio, just couldn't be a port in China, could it?

He looked down to the short-answer questions. According to Roger's key, Alexander the Great was *plucked and sautéed*? He died at a young age due to *blanched nuts*? Elizabeth I was the greatest Cream of Tartar, because she was whipped thoroughly by the Spanish Armada? "What's going on here?!?" Doug asked himself. "This is the craziest answer sheet ever! That Roger! He *cheated* me!"

"Doug?" Shocked to realize that he was still taking a test, Doug looked up. "Are you okay?" It was Mr. Mayonnaise, speaking from the front of the room.

"Y-y-yes, sir," Doug said quietly, regaining his composure.

"I don't know what's eating you, Doug, but you need to be quiet. Everybody is working very hard, and your mumbling is a distraction."

"Yes, sir," he replied. "I'm sorry."

Doug's stomach sank as he realized what his dad meant when he said that cheaters only cheat themselves. Here I am, angry at Roger for cheating me, while I'm cheating on the test! I just can't do this. If I get a bad grade, I'll get it honestly, he thought.

The questions were hard, but Doug was surprised to find that he knew a lot of the answers! He felt pretty good about it, all in all. But the bell rang before he finished.

As he left the classroom, Doug handed Roger the answer key and

said, "Here, Roger, I'd have done a lot better without this. Your answers were all wrong. They just slowed me down."

Roger's face paled. "Whaddaya mean, Funnie? These are straight from the source. How could they be wrong?"

Doug replied coolly, "I don't know, Roger, but next time, try flipping a coin. You might get a better grade."

EPILOGUE

Dear Journal,

I guess I knew more than I thought I did. All those short little study sessions really paid off.

Roger and his gang got caught; all the teachers had disguised their tests just in case anybody broke into the computer system. Roger's answers were for the home economics exam!

The only thing I can't understand is how Roger could have believed that Socrates was killed by being forced to marinate for four hours!